Find Your Fabulous

Written by Vie Portland

Illustrated by Lottie Thomson

Please share any photos or videos of you with the book with Vie, or by using #FindYourFabulous on your posts.

Though most characters in this book are fictional, there are some children featured whose parents or carers have given us permission to use their likeness for the images.

Hardback ISBN: 978-1-8384274-5-0
Paperback ISBN: 978-1-8384274-6-7
Ebook ISBN: 978-1-8384274-7-4

Book design by Dr Jennifer Jones
www.ewc.coach

First published in the UK 2024

We live in a wonderfully diverse world, with lots of different cultures, races, religions and abilities. It can be easy to focus on our differences. However, I think we all have in common the most important things for any human: we all want to feel loved, to feel happy, and to feel we belong.

In this book, there are lots of children. They all look very different. They all have people and things they love. They all have varied life experiences. Some are disabled and some are non-disabled. And they all have one amazing, incredible, joyful thing in common: they are all fabulous, just as they are.

I am a confidence and self-esteem coach and have been working with children, young people, and adults for a very long time, and I have seen how hard it is for most of them to believe in themselves, to see themselves as the wonderful beings they are. I was one of those people, too, until I started working on believing how brilliant I am.

This book demonstrates some of the work I do with young children. There is silliness and songs, but the meaning is serious, because it's far easier to boost a child's self-esteem when they're young, than repair it when they're an adult.

We all deserve to feel great about ourselves and this book is a way for all readers to see that. So, join in with me, and say it loud:

I am fabulous!

Love, Vie
xx

To every person reading this book, you deserve to feel fabulous! Celebrate who you are, as you are, because you are wonderful.

To every person who supports me, thank you for encouraging and joining in with my fabulousness.

Love, Vie

To my fabulous son Isaac and to all the children who haven't seen many characters who look like them in book illustrations, in films or on tv.

You are important and I hope you find somebody who looks a little bit like you in the pages of this book.

Lottie

Scan this code to read the Book with Vie and sing along, too! You can also access the BSL signed video of the book.

Scan this code to learn more about charities and other organisations that help people with the conditions children in this book live with every day.

FIND YOUR
FABULOUS!

Some days we can feel a little sad, or a little angry,

or a little worried,

or a little quiet.

All of those feelings
are normal!
It's important we
feel our feelings.

When we feel those things,
it's good to talk about them,
to learn why we feel them.

But sometimes we don't
know why!

Sometimes we
want to feel happy,
but it feels difficult
to remember how.

At those times we need to...

First, we're going to do some breathing.

We breathe all the time, and that's fabulous already!

But we're going to do some animal breathing!

Let's start with a snake!
We're going to take a deep breath in, and ...

as we hiss our breath out,
we're going to wiggle.

Now let's do a bee.

We take a deep breath in, then ...

as we breathe out, we're going to buzz
and wiggle our fabulous fuzzy bottoms,

just like bees do.

Next, let's do a lion!

Take a really big breath in, then ...

as we breathe out, do the biggest roar we can!

how did that feel?

Sometimes, it might not be a good time to do animal breathing out loud.

But we can still do the deep breath in and breathe out, and imagine ourselves being a slithering snake, a buzzing bee, or a roaring lion.

How do you think other animals
would do deep breaths?

Now, let's start thanking our amazing bodies for everything they do.

Thank you arms for allowing me to hug!

Thank you mouth for allowing me to sing!

Thank you bottom for allowing me to wiggle!

Thank you tummy for looking after my food!

What else could you thank your body for?

Then we can remind ourselves of
all the brilliant things we are.

How else are you fabulous?

It's good to say thank you to other people
that make us happy, too.

What else could you thank people for?

Now, we're going to sing a song!*

I love myself
as I am,
as I am!

I love myself
as I am,
as I am!

And I believe
that being me
is great!

I love myself
as I am,
as I am!

*Sung to the tune of "Head, shoulders, knees and toes"

Can you sing it in a **big voice?**

Can you sing it in a quiet voice?

Sing it often to remind yourself you are loved!

If you're having a day where
you can't remember
how fabulous you are,
ask someone to sing
the song for you.

I love you
as you are,
as you are.

I love you
as you are,
as you are.

And I believe
that you
are really
great!

I love you
as you are,
as you are.

You could also sing it
to someone who has
forgotten they are fabulous.

Who do you love?

Why do you love them?

What are great ways to show love?

What do you love?

Why do you love it?

Can you share what you love sometimes?

What is kindness?

How do you show kindness?

Who are you kind to?

Who is kind to you?

How can you be kind to someone you love?

How can you be kind to someone you don't know?

How can you be kind to yourself?

Time for another fabulous song!

If you're happy
and you know it,
give yourself a hug.
Big hug!

If you're happy
and you know it,
give yourself a hug.
Big hug!

If you're happy
and you know it,
and you really
want to show it,
if you're happy
and you know it,
give yourself a hug.

Big hug!

If you're happy
and you know it,
thank your brain.
Thank you brain!

If you're happy
and you know it,
give a big smile.
Cheese!

If you're happy
and you know it,
wiggle yourself.
Wiggle, wiggle.

If you're happy
and you know it,
shout I'm fabulous.
I'm fabulous!

Now practise saying these:

Questions and activities

You could answer these questions with your words, in drawings, in stories, in dance, or any way you would like to.

1. Draw or write down all the ways you are fabulous.

2. Give someone you love a card or letter telling them why they are fabulous.

3. Write little notes or draw happy pictures and leave them for people you don't know to find, maybe by hiding them in library books or on a bench.

4. Write a feeling-good-about-yourself song, or learn a happy dance, and teach it to someone else.

5. How do you think we can make the world kinder, so everyone feels they belong, and that they are loved? What would you do first?

Fabulous children!

Several of the children in this book told me how they are fabulous! Here's what they said:

Leo. "I am fabulous because I am defying my condition every day and me and my family are so proud."

Reuben. "I am fabulous because I am unique and full of fun and I make people smile."

Amelia. "I am fabulous because I make people giggle."

Elizabeth. "I am fabulous because I am kind, willing to try new things, and funny."

Sophia. "I am fabulous because I am me and I am creative."

Tristan. "I am fabulous because I am really kind and thoughtful."

Finlay. "I am fabulous because I am fearless and adventurous which gives my twin brother lots of confidence too."

Arthur. "I am fabulous because I make everyone smile with my cheeky personality and gorgeous dimples."

Lily. "I am fabulous because I am loving and caring especially towards my twin sister."

Poppy. "I am fabulous because I am loving and caring especially towards my twin sister."

Zeke. "I am fabulous because I am full of love!"

Elijah. "I am fabulous because I make everyone smile."

Dylan. "I am fabulous because I have inspired so many to fight EB*."

Katie. "I am fabulous because I have an incredibly kind heart and free spirit."

Josh. "I am fabulous because my enthusiasm is infectious."

Finley. "I am fabulous because I love to make everybody smile."

April. "I am fabulous because I help and care for people. I am kind."

William. "I am fabulous because I brighten up other peoples' days!"

*EB is Epidermolysis Bullosa, a rare genetic skin blistering disorder.

Romany. “I am fabulous because I can make absolutely anybody smile!”

Shailen. “I am fantastic because I make people feel happy as I am very good at making people laugh.”

Gabriel. “I am fabulous because I am very polite and chatty.”

Maebh. “I am fabulous because I am kind, friendly & brave, and when others are sad I cheer them up.”

Aoife. “I am caring, clever and I have a magic personality.”

Suerene. “I am fabulous because I have never let my disability stop me from doing what I want to do.”

Meet the Author!

Vie Portland helps people to find their fabulous, by showing them how wonderful they are, as they are.

Vie lives with several disabilities and is passionate about encouraging inclusion, kindness, and acceptance everywhere, because she knows we all bring something unique to the world, and we all deserve to be seen, heard, and valued.

She lives in Hampshire (UK) with her fabulous cats and partner.

Meet the Illustrator!

Lottie Thomson specialises in children's illustrations that embrace individuality, celebrate our differences and promote body positivity.

Living with chronic health conditions inspires her to create work for children who don't often see themselves represented in picture books. She lives and works in Nottinghamshire (UK) with her young son, husband and three fabulous cats.

Bonus Materials

Use this QR code to find more great resources!

- Braille Sheet
- British Sign Language Worksheet
- Butterfly Colouring Sheet
- I AM Printable Affirmations
- My Body Is Incredible Worksheet

Find your fabulous!

Milton Keynes UK
Ingram Content Group UK Ltd.
UKRC031746121124
451097UK00001B/3

9781838427467